Friday

the Arapaho Boy

A Story from History

by **Marc Simmons**

illustrations by **Ronald Kil**

University of New Mexico Press • Albuquerque

Books in the
Children of the West Series

Millie Cooper's Ride

José's Buffalo Hunt

Friday the Arapaho Boy

10 09 08 07 06 05 04   1 2 3 4 5

Library of Congress Cataloging-in-Publication information

Simmons, Marc.

Friday the Arapaho boy / Marc Simmons ;

[illustrations by Ron Kil].— 1st ed.

p.   cm.

ISBN 0-8263-3609-4 (cloth : alk. paper)

1. Friday (Arapaho Indian)—Juvenile literature.

2. Arapaho Indians—Biography—Juvenile literature.

[1. Friday (Arapaho Indian)

2. Arapaho Indians—Biography.

3. Indians of North America—

Great Plains—Biography.]

I. Kil, Ronald R., 1959–   ill.   II. Title.

E99.A7F75 2004

978.004'97354'0092—dc22

2003027626

Series design by Robyn Mundy

Book composition by Kathleen Sparkes

Body type is Trump Mediaeval 11.5/14

Display type is Dolmen and Freestyle 521

For
Matt Praisner
Who likes stories of
The Old West

Sweetwater R.

Fitzpatrick
and Friday
rendezvous with trappers

N. Platte R.

LAKOTA

CHEYENNE

ARAPAHO

UTE

Huerfano
Butte

Mexican
Territory

Black-spot
Found by
Fitzpatrick

KIOWA

Taos

PLAINS
APACHE

Santa
Fe
San
Miguel

COMANCHE

The Arapaho Country
and Beyond
1831

PAWNEE

Santa Fe Trail

Independence

Boones Lick

St. Louis

Missouri

OSAGE

Arkansas R.

Cimarron R.

N

RONALD KIL

Foreword

In the language of the Arapaho Indians, his name was Warshinun. In English that meant Black-spot. At age nine, the small, skinny boy called Black-spot was living with his father, mother, and younger sister in a tepee, or hide tent shaped like a cone.

Usually the Arapahos moved their tepees over the plains of eastern Colorado and parts of Kansas. They lived by hunting antelope, elk, and buffalo. But this year the herds were seldom to be found.

For two seasons little rain had fallen on the plains. No grass grew. The hungry animals drifted south looking for something to eat.

RK

lack-spot's father, Neisa-na, took his son's hand and said:
"This evening you will go with me to the council tepee.
Our elders are meeting there. They will decide where we should
go in search of fresh meat."

A fire burned in the center of the large tepee. Old and wise men
of the tribe sat in a circle upon buffalo robes. Black-spot snuggled
close to his father. He listened for hours to the council talk.

Several leaders said that the Arapahos should move south,
following the game animals. Beyond the Cimarron River (in
Oklahoma) their hunters would surely find food enough for the
whole tribe.

Others objected. "The Cimarron is deep in the land of our
enemies, the Kiowas and Apaches," they warned. "Our village
will not be safe when the young men are out hunting."

After much argument, the elders agreed to pull down the
tepees at dawn and start south into enemy country. They had
no choice. But by the time that decision was made, Black-spot
had fallen asleep.

By the whiteman's calendar, it was the last week of May 1831.
The Arapahos had traveled slowly over the blistered plains for three weeks.
Now they were camped on a sandy flat beside the Cimarron River.

Black-spot looked down into the wide bed of the Cimarron. It was
nearly dry. Only here and there could he see shallow pools of water. But he
knew there was enough for the tepee village and its large herd of horses.

During the first few days on the river, Arapaho hunters brought in
a number of antelope. They also killed an old buffalo bull, found alone
on the plains.

The buffalo meat was tough and hard to chew, Black-spot decided.
But at least everyone went to sleep at night with a full stomach.

Each morning the elders sent out scouts to search the wide land for
any sign of the Arapahos' enemies. All knew that the tribe was trespassing
on the hunting grounds of others.

Black-spot was happy here on the Cimarron. As usual, the Arapaho village hummed with activity.

He liked to watch the men making arrows and bows of Osage orange-wood. When they painted their war shields, he would sit fascinated as the deer hair brushes spread the pretty colors on the thick buffalo hide.

Sometimes Black-spot helped his mother, Néina, carry in firewood from the edge of the river. But much of the day, he played wild and free, like other Arapaho children.

One afternoon Black-spot was bored. So he took his bow and arrows and began walking up the Cimarron. He was looking for a colony of prairie dogs.

These plump little animals were not dogs at all. They were rodents, like squirrels, who lived in holes underground. Arapaho boys spent long hours hunting prairie dogs.

Black-spot hoped he could get one before dark. Then, like a good hunter, he could carry it back to the tepee for his mother to cook at supper.

Usually prairie dogs were plentiful upon the surrounding plains. But today none could be seen.

After several hours of searching, Black-spot gave up and sat down on the river bank. Just below him was a deep pool of water. Since he was hot and tired, he jumped in for a swim. While he splashed and played, another hour passed by.

At last Black-spot started back for the Arapaho camp. He broke into an easy run, remembering how far he had to go. Mile after mile, his thin little legs propelled him on.

Then, as day faded, he came to the top of a prairie swell that looked down upon the village. Black-spot stopped with a jolt and gasped.

The Arapahos and their tepees were gone!

he boy could scarcely believe his eyes. Where was his family? Where had his people gone? And why had they left so quickly in the few hours he was away?

Black-spot raced down to the sandy flat. He wanted to be sure he had come back to the right place on the river. Yes, there were the black fire pits and the circles of holes punched in the ground by tepee poles. This was the campsite, all right.

A chill went down his spine. He felt a tiny flicker of fear. Then he brushed it aside, like a good Arapaho, and began figuring out what to do.

His first thought was that game had been found south of the Cimarron and the camp had packed up and set out in that direction.

But when he looked, Black-spot could find no trail left by a moving village.

He found such a trail going north, however. That was bad news. It could mean only one thing. Their scouts had discovered enemies nearby, and the Arapaho elders decided to lead the tribe back the way they had come only a few days before.

In the bustle and confusion of leaving, Neisa-na and Néina might have been unaware that their son was missing from the village. Black-spot had told no one that he was going prairie dog hunting. Now he very much regretted his mistake.

Day was ending. As tired as he was, Black-spot felt eager to start running after the retreating village. But he knew that as soon as darkness fell, he would not be able to see the trail.

Better to crawl into the willow thicket by the river and sleep. At the first light of dawn, he could set out. With luck, he would soon meet some of his people returning to look for him.

Almost at once, the weary little boy fell fast asleep. A lone coyote barked at the stars.

Black-spot awoke early in the morning, hungry and thirsty.
He had nothing to eat, but he crept down to the river bed and
took a long drink from a pool.

Just as he got back to the willow thicket, he heard the pounding
of horses' hooves. Looking across the Cimarron, his blood froze.
Riding straight towards him was a large party of strange Indians,
carrying weapons and wearing war paint.

Without being told, Black-spot knew they were enemies of his
people. At once he threw himself on the ground and then crawled
into a dense pocket of weeds and willows.

The strangers on horseback rode right through the thicket. They passed so close to the trembling Black-spot that he could smell the sweat on their horses. But he was well hidden and no one saw him.

The riders stopped on the sandy flat beyond to study the fire pits and tepee circles. Then they galloped on north following the path of the Arapahos.

Peering from the willow bushes, the boy watched them disappear over the edge of the plains. But a few moments later, he had a scary thought: "Oh, those men are in front of me now. I can't follow the trail to find father and mother."

Black-spot was stuck on the Cimarron with no place to go.

The Arapaho boy remained in hiding throughout the day, growing hungrier by the hour. Who were these enemies, he wondered. Kiowas? Apaches?

One thing he was sure about. They were not Pawnees. Once he had seen several Pawnees raiding the Arapaho horse herd. All had shaved heads. The enemies he had glimpsed today wore long hair.

It grew late. Dark shadows stretched over the land. Sun Father dipped below the western horizon. Troubled and fearful, Black-spot prepared to spend his second night alone on the Cimarron.

Not knowing what else to do, the boy stayed where he was. He believed that sooner or later his father would come for him. If he moved on, Neisa-na might never find him.

Soon the hunger in Black-spot's belly turned to a dull ache. By the third day, he felt only weakness. Finally, he began to have visions and see things that were not really there.

Several times he believed he was riding a pony over the plains. He came to his tepee standing alone and went inside. There his mother had a pot of antelope stew bubbling on the fire.

But every time the hungry boy reached for some stew, the vision disappeared and he was suddenly by himself again on the Cimarron.

After seven days, Black-spot no longer had visions. He was too weak to go for water. He couldn't even tell day from night.

Life seemed to be slipping away. Death was looking for him. He would soon be on his way to the spirit world.

The tall man called Tom Fitzpatrick roamed widely across the western plains and mountains. He made his living as a trapper and Indian trader. All mountain men and most Indians knew his name.

In the spring of 1831, he joined a wagon caravan, leaving Independence, Missouri. Merchants in the caravan were taking trade goods over the long Santa Fe Trail to New Mexico.

Weeks later, the wagons crossed a scorched brown plain in the far corner of Kansas. Tom Fitzpatrick rode ahead, hoping to find water in the Cimarron River.

He did discover the shallow pools that the Arapaho had recently been using. And, he found something else that quite surprised him!

What tribe are you?

"Well. What on earth do we have here," exclaimed Tom Fitzpatrick. He was looking down at the small, still figure of an Indian boy, lying in a weedy willow thicket.

The tall man took his canteen from the saddle horn and stepped down from his horse. He wet a red handkerchief and rubbed the cool cloth on the child's forehead.

Black-spot's eyelids fluttered open. Startled, he looked into the large white face above. At first, he thought he had died and gone to the home of Sun Father.

But then the man lifted his head and gave him a long drink. He asked Black-spot what he was called and the name of his tribe.

The questions were made with the hands, using the Indian sign language. That language was known to all the Plains people.

Black-spot understood perfectly. But being afraid, he made no reply. The whiteman placed a small piece of dried antelope meat in his mouth, and the boy chewed it slowly. He swallowed. Exhausted, his eyes closed again and he knew nothing more for several hours.

When Black-spot awoke late in the afternoon, he was startled to find himself lying in some kind of large wooden box. White cloth arched over his head, shutting out the sky.

He had never seen a covered wagon before. Indeed, he had not seen a whiteman until today, although Black-spot at times heard his father speak of them.

Now he thought of the one who had found him on the riverbank. This "Tall Man," as he named him in Arapaho, surely meant him no harm.

What are you called?

The large wagon train from Missouri had parked in a circle next to the Cimarron. At the campfire, Tom Fitzpatrick stirred a big pot of rich soup.

A couple of the bearded wagon drivers joined him at the fire. "Well, Tom," said one. "Looks like that starving boy you brought in this morning is gonna have a mighty fine dinner."

"Yes," agreed Fitzpatrick. "This meat soup should be just the thing to make him strong again."

"Did you find out his name, Tom?" the other driver asked.

"He wouldn't or couldn't tell me," was the reply. "But since we have to call him something, I'll name him 'Friday.' That's what today is."

Later Black-spot gobbled down bowl after bowl of thick soup. Tall Man stood beside him and spoke words that the boy did not understand.

"So, young Friday. We have no choice. You'll have to travel with me for a while. Maybe up the trail somewhere, we can learn where you belong."

The Arapaho lad, now known as Friday, wondered what was about to happen to him. For sure, his life had turned onto a strange path.

The following morning Tall Man found a tough little pony for Friday to ride. The wagon train hitched up its mules and began moving over the trail. And a small Indian boy's pony trotted along. Friday was happy to be alive and no longer hungry.

For three weeks, the wagons rolled steadily toward the southwest.

The plains were left behind. Blue mountains rose on the skyline ahead.

Friday was enjoying himself. Each morning he jumped from his blankets and ran to help with the camp chores. The mule drivers let him join in hitching the animals to the wagons. They joked and laughed as they worked. Friday soon lost his fear of whitemen.

One day Tall Man said to the boy:

"Well, young fellow, you seem mighty happy now. Just wish I knew where you came from."

This time he got an answer. With a fist, Friday tapped his chest near the heart. Tall Man smiled, for he recognized that sign. Friday was an Arapaho.

I am Arapaho

When the wagons finally rumbled into Santa Fe at the end of the trail, Friday was filled with curiosity. The sights and sounds of the town with its streets and adobe houses and crowds of people amazed him. It was all so different from his own tepee village.

The Indian boy did not have long to observe and explore. A few days after their arrival, Tall Man saddled his horse and put a bridle on Friday's pony. They rode out of Santa Fe, headed for Taos, 75 miles away.

Crossing over the mountains, the pair reached Taos in three days. Friday noticed at once that the place was smaller than Santa Fe. And he saw whitemen there who were dressed in buckskin clothes, almost like Indians.

Pointing to them, Tall Man told him, "Those are fur trappers. We call them mountain men."

"I wish Neisa-na and Néina were here with me," Friday thought to himself. He wanted to share with them everything he was seeing.

om Fitzpatrick had business here in Taos. He was putting together a trading expedition. His plan was to carry supplies on muleback up the Rocky Mountains and trade them to trappers for furs.

Since Tall Man was busy, Friday got the chance to look around. In the open square, or plaza, at the center of Taos, he watched horsemen, wagons, and ox carts go by. Long-eared donkeys, with stacks of firewood piled on their backs, waited patiently until a customer bought the wood from their owners.

A few Indians came and went as well. Some were Pueblos who lived nearby. Others were Utes whose camps lay in the distant mountains. Knowing that the Utes were enemies of his people, Friday decided: "I better not let them see me."

Beaver

Buffalo

Otter

Furs for

At last, Tall Man was ready to travel. He had hired helpers to pack the mules each day and to handle the animals on the long trail north.

The mountain men, he knew, would be waiting for the beaver traps he brought them, along with the blankets, shirts, knives, gunpowder, hatchets, salt, sugar, and everything else they needed.

Friday was glad to be leaving Taos. He had spent his life on the plains with his family. Now, starting back into open country with Tall Man, he happily sang aloud an Arapaho hunting song.

Hay-a-a-ah,

I go with my bow and arrows

Hay-a-nah.

I ride my pony

Looking for buffalo.

Hay-a-ah. Yah!

Trade Goods

The long mule train guided by Tom Fitzpatrick made its way north along the foot of the Rockies. On the right, the plains stretched eastward to the horizon where Sun Father rose each day.

One afternoon they suddenly came to a stream of cold water rushing from the mountains. Friday let out a whoop.

"I know this place," he shouted to the wind. "My people often camp here." Then he grew sad. Not a single tepee could he see anywhere.

Friday and the whitemen rode past a lone hill near the stream. Tall Man called it Huerfano Butte. They were now in central Colorado, the traditional range of the Arapahos. But lack of rain and poor hunting had driven them away.

A week later, the Fitzpatrick party crossed into Wyoming and soon found the mountain men.

The trading for furs took only a short time. Friday helped Tall Man lay out on the ground the knives, traps, blankets, and everything else. The mountain men brought beaver skins they had trapped. They used the skins like money to buy the goods they needed.

To each one, Tall Man asked the same question: "Have you heard of an Arapaho family that's lost a boy?" But no one had.

When the trading was done, Tall Man Fitzpatrick paid off his helpers. Then he and Friday started overland for St. Louis far to the east.

By now, young Friday had learned many words in English. He could speak with Tall Man in simple sentences, using sign language less and less.

One day he asked Tall Man, "Why are we going to this whiteman's village, St. Louis?"

And Tom Fitzpatrick answered, "Well, my friend Friday, I'm putting you in school there. You will learn many useful things and be well cared for until I can find your parents."

Friday, the Arapaho, had no idea what a school was. But he would soon find out.

Weeks later Tall Man and Friday reached the little town of
Independence on the Missouri River. They put their horses out to
pasture on a nearby farm, then walked down to the river landing.

There a steamboat was tied up at the dock. Two large pipes in the
center of the boat belched black smoke into the air.

Of all the new things Friday had seen recently, this was the most
frightening. Tall Man took his hand and they went on board. "Don't
be afraid, little man," he said.

The "floating house" cast off and moved into the river current. The
man and the boy stood at the rail watching the tree-lined shore drift by.

Friday enjoyed his ride so much, he soon forgot his fear.

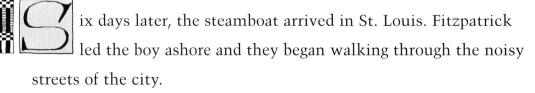ix days later, the steamboat arrived in St. Louis. Fitzpatrick led the boy ashore and they began walking through the noisy streets of the city.

Friday's eyes grew wide at the sight of so much traffic. There were fancy carriages, buggies and delivery carts. People of all kinds hurried by on important errands. A few of them were Indians, but they looked nothing like Arapahos.

A half hour's walk brought Tall Man and Friday to a great stone building surrounded by open space, grass, and trees. It was the school, a boarding school where students lived while going to class.

Inside, they were greeted by a small man with a jolly face, dressed in black. He and Fitzpatrick stepped aside and talked for a while. Then Fitzpatrick gave the man a handful of gold coins.

Tall Man said to Friday, "This will be your home for now. I'll come back and see you in a few days." Then he left.

St. Louis

RK

Tom Fitzpatrick visited several St. Louis men involved in the fur trade. He paid off some old debts and bought new supplies for his next trip to the Rockies.

At the end of the week, he returned to the school. The first thing he saw was Friday, running and kicking a ball with boys his age.

Tall Man gave a signal and Friday left the group and hurried to his side. Tall Man spoke slowly, and signed with his hands, too. He wanted to make sure the boy understood him.

"Tomorrow I leave for the mountains," he said. "I won't be back for a year or more. I'll be looking for your family. So you must remain here and wait for me."

Friday nodded, then watched his friend disappear up the street. He suddenly felt lost and sad. It was the same feeling he had on the Cimarron when his tribe left him behind.

Fitzpatrick did stay in the Rockies almost a year. But he never forgot about little Friday back in St. Louis.

Black-spot's parents had not forgotten him either. As the Arapahos wandered over the plains, his father asked everyone they met about news of his lost son.

In time Tom Fitzpatrick heard that a certain band of Arapahos had a child missing. He felt sure that it was his Friday.

One sunny morning Tall Man showed up on the steps of the St. Louis school. "I think I have found your people," he told the much-changed Friday.

The boy now spoke perfect English, wore a school uniform, and had a whiteman's haircut. He had made friends and at first was not eager to leave his new life.

He and Tall Man had a serious talk. "Friday, you have learned valuable things here," said Fitzpatrick. "But now it is time to rejoin the Arapahos."

The boy grew sorrowful. Then he thought of his father, mother, and sister and how much he missed them. That very night they left St. Louis for the West.

Six weeks passed. A much grown-up Friday rode a fine-stepping horse next to Tall Man.

Ahead of them, the grassy plains lapped up against the foot of the Shining Mountains, as the Indians called the Rockies. Suddenly, the riders came to a dip in the plain and looked down upon Arapaho tepees.

Friday's heart almost stopped, he was so excited. There was his village, much as it had looked on the Cimarron when he last saw it so long ago.

He caught a glimpse of his family's tepee. The large horse herd grazed close by. Dogs barked. Friday smelled the familiar wood smoke from the cooking fires.

Neisa-na and Néina both caught sight of the strange boy coming towards them on a prancing horse. In another moment, they recognized their own Black-spot.

Joy swept over Friday. A lump rose in his throat and tears clouded his eyes. In a high voice, he yelled in Arapaho: "I'm home at last!"

Black Spot
(Warshinun)
Friday

Afterword

riday grew up to become an important man among the Arapahos. As a warrior chief, he attended the famous council in Wyoming that led to the Fort Laramie Treaty of 1851. Tom Fitzpatrick was there and the two friends had long talks.

In later years, Friday struggled to keep his people at peace with the whiteman. By 1878 many of the Arapahos were confined on the Wind River Reservation in western Wyoming.

Black-spot, known as Friday, died in 1881, at about the age of 59. He was greatly missed, because at the time of his death he was the only Arapaho who spoke English. No whiteman then could speak the Arapaho language.

Sources

Traveler Rufus B. Sage met Friday on the Santa Fe Trail in 1844 and gave the first written account of his rescue by Fitzpatrick in the book *Scenes in the Rocky Mountains*, published in 1846. Other frontiersmen also recorded their encounters with Friday. Author LeRoy R. Hafen collected all the known sources and wrote a sketch of Friday's life that appeared in his biography, *Broken Hand: The Life of Thomas Fitzpatrick* (1973).

Sister M. Inez Hilger's *Arapaho Child Life and Its Cultural Background* (Bureau of American Ethnology, 1952), contains photographs of some of Friday's twentieth-century descendants, who continue to use "Friday" as their last name. Another valuable book is by tribal member Althea Bass, *The Arapaho Way: A Memoir of an Indian Boyhood* (1966).